Anonymous

A Southern Winter-Wreath,

culled for the motherless

Anonymous

A Southern Winter-Wreath,
culled for the motherless

ISBN/EAN: 9783337254452

Printed in Europe, USA, Canada, Australia, Japan

Cover: Foto ©Andreas Hilbeck / pixelio.de

More available books at **www.hansebooks.com**

A SOUTHERN WINTER–WREATH,

CULLED FOR THE MOTHERLESS.

CAMBRIDGE:
PRINTED AT THE RIVERSIDE PRESS.
1866.

DEDICATION.

PARENTLESS and portionless ones! Children of our Orphan's Home! For you we have gathered together and bound in a garland a little medley of Poesy and Rhyme, which has welled out in some moment of agony from the stricken heart of the sorrowing, or been cast forth in some gladsome hour of mirth by the prosperous and gay; in either case, the writers little dreaming that these waifs of the brain, scattered or lost, would be made, by passing through the mill of benevolence, into grain, to be garnered, as the staff of life for a time, for those who, like lilies of the valley and the grass of the field, toil not, neither do they spin, and yet their Heavenly Father careth for them, and heareth them when they cry, supplying all their need.

PREFACE.

THE following original pieces have been written by some of the ladies and gentlemen of Savannah, and are published for the benefit of the Episcopal Orphans' Home in that city. There are also several pieces written by friends not of the city, which have been kindly contributed.

SAVANNAH, *January*, 1866.

CONTENTS.

———

	PAGE
ON THE BIRTH OF A SON	1
PRAYER TO THE PITYING SAVIOUR	3
BID ME COME TO THEE	5
THE PASSION-FLOWER	7
MUSINGS	9
A CASTLE IN THE AIR	11
TO CAROLINE, ON PRESENTING A " REGARD RING ".	13
LINES SUGGESTED BY A VISIT TO BUONAVENTURE, IN 1834.	14
THOU HAST BORNE AWAY MY BEAUTIFUL	16
LINES ADDRESSED TO A NIGHT JESSAMINE	19
LINES ADDRESSED TO THE REV. MR. W——	21
HAST EVER LOOKED FOR MORNING-STAR WHEN FLED?	22
THE MOTHER AND HER CHILD	23
THE SABBATH	25
LINES BY THE REV. I. LORING WOART	26
LINES ON THE DEATH OF THE REV. EDWARD NEUFVILLE, D. D.	29
LINES WRITTEN ON CHRISTMAS-DAY	31
TO ——	33
THERE'S A WEE LITTLE THING	35
SOMEBODY'S DARLING	37
THE SABBATH	40
TO A " LITTLE FACE "	41
THE STAR AND THE FLOWER	44
ON THE DEATH OF ——	46

	PAGE
THE VILLAGE CHURCH	49
TO OUR IMPRISONED ONE	55
LINES SENT WITH AN ENGAGEMENT-RING	57
"ARE YOU GOD'S WIFE?"	62
TO A SOLDIER'S DOG	65
THE LAY OF THE SUNBEAM	68
TO A FRIEND, ON HER MARRIAGE	71
OUR BROTHER	74
THE PRESENT	76
JUDGE NOT	78
SUCH IS LIFE	81
OUR PASTOR	83
THE GUARDIAN ANGEL	85
LINES ON THE DEATH OF THE WRITER OF THE "VILLAGE CHURCH"	88
BEFORE THE WAR	90
AFTER THE WAR	92
LINES TO A YELLOW JESSAMINE	95
LINES BY AN OFFICER TO THREE LADIES	96
LINES ON THE SENSITIVE PLANT	97
TO THE OLD YEAR	99

On the Birth of a Son.

BY THE LATE PRESIDENT DAVIES.

THOU little wondrous miniature of man,
    Formed by unerring Wisdom's perfect
        plan;
Thou little stranger from eternal night,
Emerging into life's immortal light;
Thou heir of worlds unknown,—thou candidate
For an important, everlasting state,
Where this young embryo shall its powers ex-
        pand,
Enlarging, ripening still, and never stand.
This glimmering spark of being, just now struck
From nothing by the all-creating Rock,
To immortality shall flame and burn,
When suns and stars to native darkness turn;
Thou shalt the ruins of the world survive,
And through the rounds of endless ages live.
Now thou art born into an anxious state
Of dubious trial for thy future fate;

Now thou art listed in the war of life, —
The prize immense, and oh, severe the strife !
Another birth awaits thee, when the hour
Arrives that lands thee on the eternal shore ;
(And oh ! 't is near, with winged haste 't will
          come, —
Thy cradle rocks toward the neighboring tomb ;)
Then shall immortals say, " A son is born,"
While thee, as dead, mistaken mortals mourn ;
From glory then to glory thou shalt rise,
Or sink from deep to deeper miseries ;
Ascend perfection's everlasting scale,
Or still descend from gulf to gulf in hell.

Thou embryo angel, or thou infant fiend,
A being now begun, but ne'er to end,
What boding fears a father's heart torment,
Trembling and anxious for the grand event,
Lest thy young soul, so late by Heaven bestowed,
Forget her Father and forget her God ! —
Lest, while imprisoned in this house of clay,
To tyrant lusts she fall a helpless prey !
And lest, descending still from bad to worse,
Her immortality should prove her curse !

Maker of souls ! avert so dire a doom,
Or snatch her back to native nothing's gloom !

Prayer to the pitying Saviour.

PRAYER to the pitying Saviour,
　　That I may bear my part
　　With meek, unmurmuring spirit,
Though it be with a broken heart.
Praise for the hand that led me,
　　Through my dark and weary way,
From the valley in the shadow
　　Up to the glorious day.

Prayer to the dear Redeemer,
　　An earthly Mother's child,
Yet gentle and pure and holy,
　　Unstained and undefiled.
Praise for that tie so tender,
　　Strengthened and sanctified
In the heart of each earthly mother
　　By the blood of the Crucified.

O Father, good and gracious,
　　Who didst send down to me
An angel from Thy presence,
　　To lead me unto Thee : —

A spirit white and saintly,
  Loving and meek and mild,
Of this lone heart a comforter,
  E'en from a little child.

And thou, O Christ the merciful,
  Who rememberedst on Thy Cross
Thy *Mother's bitter agony,*
  Fainting beneath Thy Cross,
Look on my desolation,
  " Think on " my agony,
And send the angel by Thy side,
  To " take me home " to Thee.

Bid me come to Thee.

OH, bid me come to Thee! Earth's flow-
ers are fading, —
Dying along my pathway, one by one:
Oh, bid me come to Thee! The way is dreary,
And now the stars shine not, as once they
shone.
Oh, bid me come to Thee! The tempests gather
Darkly and wild o'er my defenceless head;
My slow steps falter, for they miss the guiding
Of that clasped hand by which they once were
led.

Oh, bid me come to Thee! Glad sounds no
longer
Spring with their sudden gush of melody;
The low, sweet voice is mute, that, night and
morning,
Mingled with mine, in prayer and praise to
Thee!

Oh, bid me come to Thee! My heart is yearning
　　For the blest mansions Thou hast made my
　　　　home;
Sweet voices call me, and young angel-faces,
　　Upturned to Thee, *implore* that I may come.

A white-robed form, from my torn heart just
　　　　parted,
　　Bestrewn with lilies, wears an angel-crown;
Close to thy breast, as late to mine enfolded,
　　With pleading eyes on me looks softly down.
Part us no longer, O thou gracious Saviour, —
　　Mother and child, we lowly bend the knee;
In Thy most precious blood made white and holy,
　　Divine Redeemer, bid me come to Thee!

The Passion-Flower.

WRITTEN IN SAVANNAH, AND PRESENTED TO A FRIEND.

ILD Superstition named the flower
　　In memory of that awful hour,
　　When He, whom Heaven and Earth
　　　adore,
The death of shame and sorrow bore.

They called the purple circlet there,
The crown of thorns 't was His to bear;
And every leaf seemed to their eye
Memorial of His agony.

'T is fancy all! yet do not scorn
The thought of adoration born;
But let each flower that meets our sight
Recall the Lord of Life and Light!

There 's not one flower that decks the vale,
And with its fragrance scents the gale,

That does not bid our hearts arise
To Him who dwells beyond the skies.

In valley lone, on mountain height,
All in one common tale unite;
All speak His love, who died, that we
Might live throughout eternity.

" That higher suffering which we dread
    A higher joy discloses; —
Men saw the thorns on Jesus' brow,
    But angels saw the roses."

Musings.

WHILE musing by the fireside, —
　　The fireside of home !
How many sad and happy thoughts
　And tender memories come

Unbidden, as my heart recalls
　The checkered years gone by !
Poor heart ! now throbbing wild with joy,
　Now bursting with a sigh !

Bursting with a wearied sigh,
　For the faded hopes that strew
Life's pathway, — like the fallen leaves
　Of roses bright with dew :

For sad and holy memories
　Of love, now lost to me !
Ah ! what a blessing was that love !
　So pure, so full, so free !

Be still, my heart, nor dare repine !
 Was 't not a Father's hand ?
Why ever seek thy springs of joy
 Within Earth's barren land ?

Nay ! look to Heaven; thy bud of love
 Hath *full fruition there !*
Where earth-stained grief nor change is known,
 Nor sorrow's ceaseless tear.

Oh, passing sweet to the weary
 Is the hope of Heaven's rest !
To-night it seems so dreary !
 Oh, soothe my troubled breast !

I long to end my lifeless dream,
 And haste me to that shore,
To meet again — ah ! blissful thought ! —
 The loved ones gone before !

A Castle in the Air.

WHEN fancy, warm with youthful fire,
Paints visions such as youth admire,
Methought my prospects bright and fair : —
'T was all a castle in the air.

With wealth I sought to fill the mind,
Bribing all cares to stay behind ;
But wealth proved nothing but a snare, —
'T was all a castle in the air.

With honors blushing all around,
I sought my warm desires to bound ;
But honors gained with toil and care
Were but as castles in the air.

From hope to hope my heart was driven,
Seeking, in vain, on Earth my Heaven ;
Nor could I yet to think forbear,
All were not castles in the air.

But nature's gloom at length gave place
To light that beamed from Sovereign grace;
My earthly castles bright and fair
All vanished into empty air.

The eye of faith was taught to soar
Beyond Time's narrow, wasting shore; —
The Spirit showed a Temple there
That was *no castle in the air.*

A. C.

To Caroline,

ON PRESENTING A "REGARD RING."

CCEPT, sweet girl, of my " Regard : "
  My aim 't will be to prove
  No spell can closer bind our hearts, —
Aye, not e'en that of love !

True love 's engendered by regard ;
  Else valueless 't would be ;
'T is this regard, fair Caroline,
  I offer now to thee.

Lines

SUGGESTED BY A VISIT TO BUONAVENTURE, IN 1834:

BY A STRANGER.

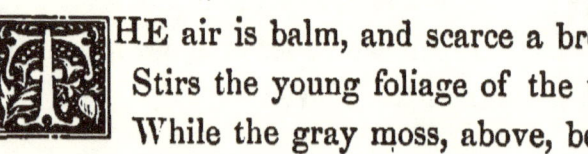

THE air is balm, and scarce a breeze
Stirs the young foliage of the trees;
While the gray moss, above, beneath,
In many a light, fantastic wreath,
A net of feathery drapery weaves,
And mingles with the glossy leaves.
Soft odors o'er the senses steal,
And many a hidden flower reveal.
Here, round the tall magnolia, twine
The rose and graceful jessamine,
With taper leaf and flow'ret fair,
Shedding its perfume on the air.
The waveless stream in silence flows,
No sound disturbs the sweet repose,
As if the world were lulled to rest,
And slept on gentle Nature's breast.

Here pause and contemplate the common doom :
Here Nature's arched Cathedral shades the tomb.

The obelisk here rises o'er the grave, —
Affection's tribute to and from the brave.
But now the air is stirred, — a breath divine
Sweeps through the woods, and o'er the distant
      pine.
I hear the voice of God among the trees,
And in the murmur of the rising breeze ;
Deep and sublime the sound, like ocean's roar,
When rising waves steal on the distant shore ;
While earth, air, ocean, with united voice,
Utter His praises, — in His smile rejoice.

Shall man alone in silence seek repose ? —
Man ! for whose sake God suffered, died, and
      rose ?
Adoring, let him humbly bend the knee,
While his rapt soul ascends, O Triune God, to
      Thee !

Thou hast borne away my Beautiful.

THOU hast borne away my beautiful,
    From her father's halls, O Death !
    Thou hast breathed upon my April
  flower
With thy chill and withering breath.
From the yearning heart, and the clinging arm,
  Where that young head loved to rest,
Thou hast borne away my cherished one
  To the cold earth's quiet breast.

Thou hast paled the ruby lip, O Death !
  Thou hast checked the merry tone, —
And I pause to hear the bounding foot
  Of my little gladsome one ;
And those deep blue eyes, with their fringed lids,
  So beautiful to me, —
I felt thy cruel hand, O Death,
  As it closed them heavily.

Thou hast crushed the tender flower, O Death,
    And spared the drooping tree;
Thou hast flung thy shadow o'er my path,
    And made earth dark to me.
My beautiful, my gentle one,
    So guileless and so mild; —
Could'st thou not spare to this poor heart
    That *little loving child?*

I feel her soft hand's gentle touch
    By my weary couch of pain,
And the tiny fingers in my hair,
    Where they ne'er may rest again, —
And that nightly prayer, with its nightly kiss,
    Oh I *hear*, I *feel* them now,
As I look upon the folded hands
    And meek uplifted brow.

I hear the gush of the merry song
    She is singing at my feet;
I see her start with a joyous shout
    Her father's step to greet.
They cluster round him, — that little band, —
    And he looks on his boys with pride,
But the heart's first love, and the fond " first kiss,"
    He can give to none beside.

2

I thought to walk life's thorny path
  With thy gentle hand to guide,
Nor feared to tread death's darkened vale,
  If thou wert by my side.
But seraphs have called thee from me above,
  To share in their blissful home;
God! thou hast taken the happy *child*, —
  Let the weary mother come!

I have looked my last on that angel-face
  In its cálm and dreamless sleep,
And my heart, in its tearless agony,
  Was all too cold to weep;
But night came down o'er my fainting soul,
  As they bore thee away from me:
Oh, my *beautiful, my treasured one,*
  Would I had died for thee!

Lines

ADDRESSED TO A NIGHT JESSAMINE, THE GIFT OF A
FRIEND.

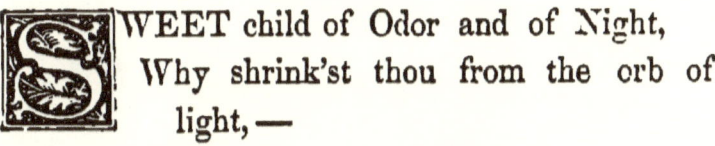

SWEET child of Odor and of Night,
　　Why shrink'st thou from the orb of
　　　light, —
And only yield'st thy rich perfume
When evening spreads her shades of gloom?

Can " Araby the Blest" dispense
A fragrance sweeter to the sense
Than thou canst shed, in thine own hour,
When music soothes with gentle power?

The sunbeams of thy natal clime
Are warmer far than those of mine ;
Yet in her wilds you bloom unseen,
And here you reign a greenhouse Queen.

While sheltered from the wintry storm,
No gale thy branches can deform,

Nor crush thy snowy flow'rets fair
That throw their fragrance on the air.

I'll nourish thee, sweet flower, with care,
And from thy branches others rear,
That when death's touch thy root assails,
Thou still shalt scent the evening gales.

Lines

ADDRESSED TO THE REV. MR. W—— BY A FEMALE
FRIEND, ON READING A SERMON OF HIS ON THE TEXT,
"AND PETER WENT OUT, AND WEPT BITTERLY."

GIFTED thou art ! yet oh, beware,
 Lest human praise thy soul ensnare :
 Keep upward fixed thine heavenward
  eye,
Nor trust its gaze beneath the sky.
Like Peter firm, — now strong in love ;
Like Peter frail, thy heart may prove :
Thy work is here, — thy home above ;
Watch in untiring prayer and love.

Hast ever looked for Morning-Star when fled?

H AST ever looked for morning-star when fled?
O r kissed the loved, and found the body dead?
P assed your .pale lips from brow to cheek or
　　hand, —
E ach moment thinking how you 've hoped and
　　planned?
L earning in portion of a dreary day,
E arth's emptiness, and cruel power to slay
S weet beings dearer to you far than life,
S paring not child, or fond and clinging wife.

I pause!   Why murmur that 't is so?
L ife ofttimes is a scene of woe.
L ingering illness tries the soul,
N eeding firm patience and control:
E nded, it brings heaven's joys to view,
S weeter for trials it has passed through,
S afer for thorns which its path did strew.

The Mother and her Child.

AIR — " *Oh, my love is like the red, red rose.*"

OH, my babe is like the red, red rose,
   Just budding on the tree!
Oh, my babe is like the lily white, —
The Queen of all the sea!

His eye is like the morning gleam,
   To weary watchers given, —
So bright, so pure its gentle beam,
   You'd think it light from heaven!

Oh, his cheek is like the downy fruit
   Just plucked from off the tree!
His lips are like the crimson glow
   Of coral in the sea.

His voice is like the morning bird's,
   That sings at Heaven's gate, —
Just like its wooing music-tone
   When calling to its mate.

Oh, his smile is like the dewy eve,
  When stars are shining gay!
His laugh is like the running stream,
  That warbles on its way.

Oh! *well* I love my bonny child!
  Could *you* his graces see,
You 'd say he was an angel mild,
  Sent down from heaven to me!

Tallulah.

The Sabbath.

WELCOME sweet day of sacred rest,
   To earthly mortals given, —
The gift divine, the rich bequest,
That links us strong to heaven!

A Sabbath stillness fills the air,
   And all is sweet repose :
The soul that 's freed from busy care
   Can pious thoughts disclose.

Then let us lift our thoughts above,
   And with the angels raise
Glad songs of holy joy and love
   To our Immanuel's praise.

Lines

BY THE REV. I. LORING WOART, WHO WAS LOST IN
THE PULASKI.

Written while at the Theological Seminary in Alexandria,
under the following circumstances: —

Hearing, one evening, a lady sing a song, "O Pescator,"
which was a favorite with himself and others, the wish was
expressed that the air might be adapted to sacred words. In
a few days he presented the subjoined lines. The peculiar
measure in which they are written was required by the music.
Had the lamented author written them under a presentiment
of the mysterious providence which awaited him, they could
not have been more touching and appropriate. The sentiments
were suggested by those memorable words of our Saviour to
his terrified disciples, " It is I."

IN notes of comfort falling,
"It is I;"
'Mid the storm in mercy calling,
"It is I,"
Our Saviour's voice once spoke,
When the tempest loudly swelling,
Fearful death to all foretelling,
In anger broke.

Though raging billows toss thee,
   " It is I ; "
Though fearful lightnings cross thee,
   " It is I "
  Can calmness yet restore :
'Mid the billows' wild commotion,
'Mid the fury of the ocean,
  Hope gleams once more.

O'er the troubled waves unmoved, —
   " It is I."
In the toilsome journey proved, —
   " It is I "
  Can fearful doubts dispel :
Still the promise-bow shall cheer thee,
Still the Saviour's arm is near thee, —
  All shall be well.

Thy spirit still upholding, —
   " It is I."
The joys of heaven unfolding, —
   " It is I "
  Can endless bliss bestow :
Crowned with blessing death shall meet thee,
Messenger of peace, to greet thee
  In love below.

'Mid the glorious songs above, —
     "It is I."
Praises of Redeeming love, —
     "It is I"
    Will give thee peaceful rest:
In my court thy home shall be;
'Mid happiness I 'll render thee
    Forever blest.

Lines

ON THE DEATH OF THE REV. EDWARD NEUFVILLE, D. D.

"*Or ever the silver cord be loosed,*" etc.   Eccl. xii. 6, 7.

LIFE'S throbbing pulse hath ceased to
      beat,
    Life's fever now is o'er;
No more shall we thy coming greet,
   As we were wont of yore;
The voice that told of joys above, —
   That did glad tidings bear, —
No more will whisper peace and love
   Unto our ravished ear.

No more the widow's heart will sing
   With joy to see thee nigh;
No more wilt thou the blessing bring
   To dry the orphan's eye.
The sufferer on his couch of pain,
   The household of the poor,
Will long for thee, *but long in vain,*
   For thou wilt come *no more.*

But nobly hast thou run thy race,
    O Brother, brave and true ;
Armed with the power of sovereign grace,
    Thou didst thy foes subdue.
The world, the flesh, the devil's snare,
    Thou trampled'st underneath,
And thine shall be the bliss to wear
    The victor's fadeless wreath.

Alas for those whom thou hast left
    In this their deep distress !
Oh, when of friend like *thee* bereft,
    Earth has no charm to bless.
Oh may they from the tempter free
    Remain till life is o'er ;
So shall they then commune with thee
    In joy for evermore.

                        Hon. Robert M. Charlton.

Lines written on Christmas-Day.

NO sunbeams gild the joyous morn
   On which our Heavenly King was born :
   A Prophet, too, and King was He,
Who groaned and died on Calvary.

The clouded sky and chilling air
Spread their deep gloom o'er scenes *once* fair ;
The moaning wind, like sorrow's sigh,
No record makes, but passes by.

It speaks of hopes that once were bright, —
Of joys, that, like the glow-worm's light,
Shed transient lustre round me here :
Then followed darkness and despair !

And what are honors now to me ?
True happiness I nowhere see ;
In vain we seek it here below, —
At every step we meet a foe !

Then look to *Him* who died to save
Poor sinners from a hopeless grave, —
To purchase pardon with the seal
Of what alone has power to heal, —

His precious blood so freely shed;
The weary pilgrim now is led
Humbly to bow before that Cross,
And deem all else but empty dross.

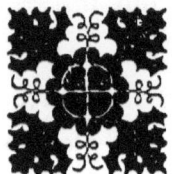

To ——.

DEAR sister! I have read thy heart
　　In these simple little flowers,
　　For sweetly does their gentle art
　Reveal such love as ours:
The snow-drop and the heart's-ease tell
The tale of sympathy full well.

Pure snow-drop! fitting emblem thou
　　Of childhood's sunny mirth;
With crown of green upon thy brow,
　　Thou leadest Spring on earth.
Frail child of Winter and of May,
Too fair thou seem'st for earth's decay!

" Clad in thy robe of spotless white "
　　Thou shalt not always be!
On thee must come the heavy blight,
　　Child of mortality!
Then must thou droop thy gentle head,
Thy tale of earthly beauty, said.

3

Our cherished snow-drop, pure and fair,
Faded from earthly view :
Eternally it bloometh now,
God's seal immortal on its brow !

Like thee, a boon of tender love,
   Was our sweet blossom given,
To lure our souls to rest above,
   Far from earth's storms, in heaven !
Sweet heart's-ease ! dost thou truly tell,
" *Where* lives thy flow'ret, thou shalt dwell " ?

There's a wee little Thing.

THERE'S a wee little thing in this world
　　　　of ours,
　　　　And it moveth and moveth the live-
long day,
And though the sun shines, and though the storm
　　　　lowers,
　　It clattereth on with its ceaseless lay.
　　　　Over peasant and king
　　　　Its spell it hath flung,
　　That dear little thing, —
　　　A lady's tongue!

There's a wee little thing in this world of ours,
　　And it throbbeth and throbbeth the livelong
　　　　day,
And in palace halls, and in leafy bowers,
　　It holdeth alike its potent sway.
　　　　Bright joy it can bring,
　　　　Or deep sorrow impart,
　　That dear little thing, —
　　　A woman's heart.

There's a wee little thing in this world of care,
  And it sparkleth and sparkleth the livelong
      day;
No dew-drop that hangs on the morning flowers
  Is so beauteous and bright as its beaming
      ray.
    No shield can we bring
      That its shaft can defy,
    That dear little thing, —
      A woman's eye!

There are many charms in this world of ours,
  That cluster and shine over life's long day;
The wealth of the mine, and the statesman's
      powers,
And the laurels won in the bloody fray:
    No spell can they fling
      That my bosom can move
    Like that witching thing, —
      A lady's love!

                Hon. Robert M. Charlton.

Somebody's Darling.

[The following are some lines written by a young lady of Savannah. Several persons have asked me to place them amidst our offerings; and I have only hesitated because the absence of the young lady prevents my asking her permission. But as they were written and published during the war I have allowed my desire to publish them to yield to my determination to insert nothing without first asking the permission of the writer. It is scarcely necessary to state that the piece was written during the war which has just closed.]

INTO a ward of the whitewashed halls,
    Where the dead and the dying lay,
    Wounded by bayonets, shells, and balls,
Somebody's darling was borne one day; —
Somebody's darling, so young and so brave !
    Wearing yet on his sweet, pale face, —
Soon to be hid in the dust of the grave, —
    The lingering light of his boyhood's grace.

Matted and damp are the curls of gold
    Kissing the snow of that fair young brow;
Pale are the lips of delicate mould, —
    Somebody's darling is *dying now*.

Back from his beautiful blue-veined brow
　　Brush his wandering waves of gold ;
Cross his hands on his bosom now, —
　　Somebody's darling *is still and cold.*

Kiss him once for *somebody's* sake,
　　Murmur a prayer both soft and low ;
One bright curl from its fair mates take, —
　　They were somebody's pride, you know.
Somebody's hand hath rested there ;
　　Was it a mother's, soft and white ?
Or have the lips of a sister fair
　　Been baptized in their waves of light ?

God knows best, — he was somebody's love ;
　　Somebody's heart enshrined him there,
Somebody wafted his name above,
　　Night and morn, on the wings of prayer.
Somebody wept when he marched away,
　　Looking so handsome, brave, and grand !
Somebody's kiss on his forehead lay,
　　Somebody clung to his parting hand.

Somebody 's watching and waiting for him,
　　Yearning to hold him again to her heart ;
And there he lies, with his blue eyes dim,
　　And the smiling, childlike lips apart.

Tenderly bury the fair young dead, —
   Pausing to drop on his grave a tear ;
Carve on the wooden slab o'er his head, —
   " Somebody's darling slumbers here."

SAVANNAH, *Jan.* 14, 1864.

The Sabbath.

'TIS the holy Sabbath morning!
    Angel voices echo near,
    And a sweet and pleasant murmur
Floats melodious through the air!
Soft the plaintive winds are sighing,
    And the breezes rustle by,
While the little birds replying,
    Lift their voices to the sky:
            So do I.

Every little leaf is tossing
    Like a gladsome child at play,
And the long-armed branches, crossing
    Like a pious saint to pray!
Earth her grassy bed discloses,
    Washed with dew-drops from on high,
And the pure and white-leaved roses
    Bare their bosoms to the sky:
            So do I.

To a " Little Face."

 HAVE been asked in sweetest tone,
Cadenced by mother's voice alone,
To write some lines, in little space,
Upon a precious " Little Face."
I shrink ! for 't would be sad disgrace
If I should fail, or should efface
By *lines*, the *charms* my pen should trace ;
But I will try to interlace
The beauties of that " Little Face."

Oh, be not jealous ! little features,
For first I speak of little creature's
Broad, open, and unspotted brow,
Innocent and unclouded now.
In after-life, if God doth spare,
Her brow will show the signs of care ;
But now, if anger or distress
Her heaving bosom doth oppress,
She screws her eyes, her nose, her lips,
Or clenches fingers to the tips.
God keep your sweet unclouded brow
E'en innocent and pure *as now.*

Now shall we take the eyes in turn,
And strive their destiny to learn?
What will those glistening orbs reveal
As they behind their fringes steal,
Closing their lids, as if to hide
What constitutes a mother's pride?
Those eyes will turn, with love to beam,
Or else will droop, their thoughts to screen.

And then the nose, — a little puggy, —
But that belongs to faces chubby:
The bone its stiffness will attain,
When years upon it quickly gain.
But while the nose is wondrous feature,
'T is not romantic, Little Creature!
So we will leave it to reform,
And beg that it will ne'er deform
The " Little Face " it rests upon,
And which it does so well become.

And now we call the mouth to speak,
And hope that 't will not in a freak
Pucker its cherry lips together,
Meditating in silence whether
It will disclose the pretty teeth
Which rest so quietly beneath
The gateway separated wide

By dimples guarding on each side,
Resting amidst the peachy down
Wherein it seems its smiles to drown.

And now the chin will not disgrace
The end of sweetest " Little Face."
Set prettily, and in right place,
The line of beauty there we trace.
But after all, description whole
Leaves out the impress of the soul.
And clustering curls, and ears like shells,
And head where brain and intellect dwells,
And rounded limbs, from nature's mould,
And hands and feet, —— Oh, I 've not told
The half of beauty I could trace
If not confined to " Little Face."

SAVANNAH, *Dec.* 18, 1865.

The Star and the Flower.

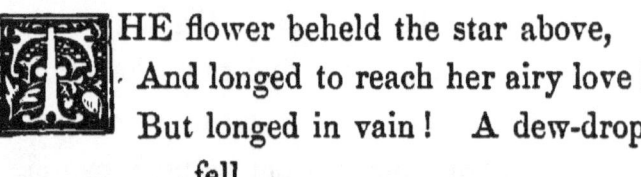HE flower beheld the star above,
And longed to reach her airy love!
But longed in vain! A dew-drop
fell
Into the soft and fragrant cell;
And then the star was imaged there,
Pure as if dropped from upper air,
And gliding down from heaven had come,
To find on earth a kindred home!
Blest was the little flower to bear
In its own breast a thing so fair!

Ah, longing eye! strain not thy gaze,
Till blinded by the golden rays
Of light, too strong for mortal's sight!
Rest thee on earth! here seek thy fill
Of beauty, in the pictured scene
Spread round, of woody hill

And verdant vale ; of Nature's mien
Swift changing with the passing shade
Of darkling cloud, and skies that fade
Too soon, from morning's promise fair !

Drink in the beauty round thee lying !
Take earth, with all its joys, — its sighing,
Its morning promise, vainly fair !
And trust to find in heaven above
What fails thee here of light and love !
Let faith and hope the dew-drops be
That mirror heaven's light to thee !

May 14, 1861.

On the Death of ——.

SAW her when a joyous thing,
With gladness ever on the wing ;
Her sparkling eyes forever flashing,
Her raven. locks forever dashing,
Like darkness on the steps of morn,
Or clouds that varying sky adorn.

I saw her in the beauteous shade
Of sweet Montpelier's hill and glade ;
I saw her girlish beauty glide
Maturing into woman's pride,
And felt that gay and buoyant heart
Would surely make a shining mark.

I saw her in the glittering crowd, —
Of adulation she was proud, —
I thought how many hearts are glad,
I thought how many hearts are sad,
And I wondered often as I gazed,
And wondered as I smiled, and praised.

I saw her, when she wearied seemed,
And wondered if she ever dreamed
That she for nobler aims must strive,
Else her gay spirit would derive
Sadness from sources all unknown,—
Sadness from God, on Love's own throne.

Again I saw her as a bride, —
A father's and a household's pride !
I saw her, and I wept to think
How many, on the very brink
Of desolation, stop to drink
Of Love's sweet fountain, but to shrink
When Death the icy hand will lay,
And tell them here, thou may'st not stay.

I saw her when keen sorrow's shade
Upon her brow sad marks had laid ;
I looked ! 't was painful, but I knew
God's child must pass e'en sorrows through,
That earthly heart He might renew,
And make through earthly beauty shine
The rays of Image all divine.

I saw her in her lovely pride,
With joyous infants by her side ;
Now she was purified, I felt

How strangely God with her had dealt.
I looked for days of joy again
To wipe away the marks of pain.

But keener sorrow yet was laid
   Upon her mother's heart;
The lovely baby round her played,
   Then clinging, had to part!
She felt that she must follow too;
But Christ alone could help him through.

Then father followed infants dead,
And o'er her soul an awe was spread:
The circle once so gay, so blest,
Seemed to be gathering to their rest.
She gave her heart to God, and plead,
As children plead for daily bread,
That He her little one would spare,
And let its life its mother's share!
God took her little one above,
And called, " Come, share my heavenly love."
And when I saw them side by side,
I knew they lived, though they had died.

SAVANNAH, *Nov.* 1865.

The Village Church.

THE morning-star, bright herald of the
    day,
    Now lifts her torch, and bares her
burning breast;
Now sinks the moon, now fade the stars away,
    Wrapped in the sable shadows of the west.

Not yet sweet morning's softened murmurs rise;
    Not yet the deer starts at the hunter's horn;
Not yet the pathways of the eastern skies
    Are printed with the rosy step of Morn.

Not yet the flowers their thousand odors fling;
    Not yet low-warbled notes the green woods
      hear;
Not yet the wild birds stretch the graceful wing,
    And float their bosoms on the sweet-breathed
      air.

4

Fresh-bursting beauties smile around unseen;
   Blue waters sweep their crescent shores un-
      heard;
No steps but mine now tread the village-green,
   No tongue wakes echo with a careless word.

Unlistened to by other ears than these,
   The matin clock chimes forth its mellow sound;
Unheeded but by me, 'mid yon dark trees,
   The village church breathes sanctity around.

Dim twilight sleeps upon its ancient eaves;
   Its moss-grown roof with dew-drops is im-
      pearled;
Its pure white sides peep through the gloomy
      leaves,
   Like Hope amidst the sorrows of the world!

Its humble spire points upward from the scene
   Of crime and care, — black blots upon life's
      page;
Around its walls wreathe curling vines of green,
   Like smiles spread on the wrinkled cheeks of
      Age.

Let gentle thought her pensive powers assume,
   Breathe inspiration from the scented breeze,

And cull a moral from each crumbling tomb
  That fills the shadows of these church-yard
    trees !

Wave on, sweet shades ! Life's passions come
    not here !
Ye list alone to heaven-aspiring hymns !
E'en schoolboys passing by, neglect to tear
  From you the nests that cradle in your limbs !

Wave on in peace ! Your lot it is to see
  Borne to their tombs the young, the gay, the
    brave ;
Your lot to mark, beneath some neighboring tree,
  The orphan weeping o'er her parent's grave.

Wave on ! No herds beneath your branches
    graze ;
  Over no common ground your green limbs
    spread ;
Ye screen from careless and unhallowed gaze
  The sad, dull, turf-piled dwellings of the dead !

Full many a loftier dome, a nobler aisle,
  And walls more beautiful than these may rise ;
Full many a statelier roof, a grander pile,
  May rear their splendid structure to the skies.

Temples there may be built with rarer art,
    Perfumed with sweeter incense from the bowl
But *thine*, the richer temple of the heart, —
    Thine is the purer incense from the soul!

Can fluted shaft, or marble-column'd hall,
    Or gilded galleries, and the arches smooth,
Answer to Him who reigns the Lord of all,
    In place of worship, humbleness, and truth?

Can He to whom globes are but grains of sand,
    Who with one nod can crush the starry crowds,
Who holds the roaring oceans in his hand,
    And robes his form in lightnings and in
        clouds, —

Who dwells where seraphs and winged angels
        hark
    To the rich music of the planets' tones,
And whose breath lit the sun's red lamp, remark
    On earth the difference of a few rude stones?

The Indian's hut, who through the wild wood
        roams,
    Though it be built of reeds, if free from sin,
He far prefers to vast cathedral domes,
    With pomp and pride and luxury within.

No pomp, no pride, no city's show is yours !
 No lisping priest here hurries through his
  task !
No heedless crowds pass through these simple
  doors,
 To cheat their follies with a sacred mask.

No actress wearied from the midnight stage,
 Here chants, for hire, the great Eternal's
  praise ;
Choirs of young lips, as fresh in heart as age,
 Swell here to Heaven their consecrated lays.

No listless audience lolls upon your seats ;
 No courteous tongue wings prayers without a
  thought ;
The hum and buzzing of the bustling streets
 Break not the worship of this peaceful spot.

  . . . . .

Farewell, sweet scene ! Day's toils have come
  again ;
 The sky's red blush now tints the rippling
  shore ;
I hear faint bleating on the far-off plain,
 And catch the plashings of the boatman's oar.

Farewell! be my last rest from life's alarm,
　　Not in the thundering surges of the seas;
Not in the city's din, but midst the calm
　　And sacred silence of such shades as these.

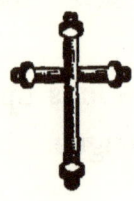

To Our Imprisoned One.

ART thou remembered, thou imprisoned
one?
Art thou remembered, when earth's
work seems done?
Thou art remembered in woman's true heart.
Sire and son to their children impart
The hopes and the fears that oft struggle within,
As they crush out the feelings that savor of sin.

Who, who can commune with his heart, and
be still? —
And yet, to do this is our dear Father's will.
Who, who, in his strength, can forgive the harsh
plan,
That placed you where sympathy from fellow-
man
May never descend on your poor, aching heart,
May never tempt care for a time to depart.

But we will have courage ! we 'll never despair !
While God is in heaven, He 'll hear earnest
    prayer.
He has not forsaken His children, we know ;
He only has chastened us, that the sharp blow
May make us a people more nearly allied
To God, *oft forgotten* in seasons of *pride !*

We remember thee often, thou imprisoned one !
When the day is just closing, or dawn has begun.
We 'll remember thee often, whatever betide,
And wish that we only could steal to thy side,
To tell thee how many hot tears have been shed,
How many brave hearts for the 'prisoned have
    bled !

And if God restores thee to country and home,
When Time on its pinions still further has flown,
The doubt of our sympathy will pass from your
    heart,
And the fear of neglect will forever depart ;
For love, though unbidden, will flow like a tide,
Giving zest to proud truth and affectionate
    pride !

OCT. 12, 1865.

Lines

SENT WITH AN ENGAGEMENT-RING, IN ANSWER TO THE QUESTION, "WHAT MADE YOU MAKE ME CHANGE MY MIND?"

T is a question asked with all the mirth-
  fulness
  Of a young heart, full of hope and fond
 anticipations
Of the happiness of future years; asked with
  that
Utter fearlessness of wrong which true love still
  inspires.
For still, towards men, as towards God, 't is true,
That "perfect love casts out all fear,"
And makes us lean with unsuspecting confidence
Upon its object. But in me, what sober thoughts
Thy question doth awaken! — Thus to find thy
  heart
Casting upon me its immeasurable wealth,
As freely as the ocean casts its wealth
Upon the embracing shore. What self-distrust
Arises, lest thou learn from me that anguish

Of ill-requited love, and tenderness misplaced,
Which many a noble woman before thee
Has found in man, in whom she dreamed to
    find it
No more than thou dream'st now. " God keep
    me
From such an evil day !" thou pray'st. And I
    pray too,
" God shield thee from such pangs !" for sooner
    would I die
Than be the one to inflict them. Yet when I
    think
What tenderness, what fond, unvarying love
A soul like thine doth long for, from the man
To whom, without reserve, it has surrendered
Its every hope of happiness on earth, —
How it doth ever afterward turn to him,
As plants turn to the sun, for light and warmth,
Gasping for kindness from him, as the thirsty
    earth
Doth gasp to the o'ershadowing cloud ;
How one harsh word from him hath grating in it
More hoarse than thunder ; and a cold look
Doth cut her soul with anguish worse than
    death !
Meditating this, what fears oppress me ! —
Fears of future tears, in secret shed,

With shiverings of the heart, and bitter grief;
Eating, unrevealed, that life which I was bound
To cherish and protect.

.   .   .   .   .

Oh but that woman makes
Adventure desperate, whoe'er she be, that trusts
Her all of happiness thus to one man's truth;
Embarking all her wealth in one ship yet un-
    tried!
Wreck if she make, thereafter naught remains
For her but hope of heaven; for from hence-
    forth
Darkness and storms and suffering settle down
Upon her sea of life, extinguishing earth's stars.
Often when I am near thee, oft when thou
    send'st
Some missive, fraught with unmistakable tokens
Of thy heart's true love; or when my memory
Recurs, as constantly it does, to all the proofs
Which thou hast given of it, — still, amid the
    joy
That overspreads my soul, like flashes of summer
    lightning,
There will come, thoughts of all that thou may'st
    suffer.
Nor can I sit beside thy mother, and observe

The tearful tenderness steal to her eye, when
    thou
Art barely mentioned, but I tremble in myself.

   .   .   .   .   .

Yet God doth know what sorrow it awakens
Within my soul, — the thought of ever being
Cause of pain to thee; and with what earnest-
    ness
I pray, that never word or look of mine
May bring tears to thine eyes, or shadows to thy
    brow.
And He who knoweth all things, knoweth
Likewise how much I love thee; and that this
It is which makes me apprehensive.

Surely then thy God will bless thee;
And, for thy sake, me.   And "thou shalt be the
    mirror
Whereat I will dress my soul."   And thy clear
    life,
Thy gentleness and many virtues seen, shall wean
The harshness from my nature; and from Heaven
Thy constant prayers and constant piety
Shall gain such grace for me, as shall secure
Thy happiness, while God shall spare us for
    each other.

   .   .   .   .

Can'st thou hope this? then, dovelike, go on
Building thy nest of love within my heart.

.   .   .   .   .

What can I do but promise thee,
With such solemnity, as if I stood already
Before God's altar, that if He will help me,
My heart shall shield thee till it cease to beat.
Or thou be taken from me into heaven?

"Are You God's Wife?"

A lady who was one day walking in one of the streets of a large city, saw a little girl looking eagerly into a large glass window, in which were displayed delightful pastry and fruits. Unobserved by the child, she went into the store, and purchased a basket, which she filled with nice things. She then went to the child, and told her to slip the basket on her arm. In amazement, the child looked up for an explanation. "Take the basket," she said; "it is for you." "And all that is in it?" asked the astonished child. "Yes, and all that is in it," the lady replied. The child raised her eyes searchingly to the lady's, and asked, "Are you God's wife?"

STANDING before a crystal screen,
 With plate-glass richly set between,
 A little child, with eager eyes,
Beheld grapes, fruits, and dainty pies,
And wondered why some never knew
The pains of hunger, as hours flew,
While many a child, with weary tread,
Begged vainly for its daily bread.

A lady entered, 'midst the crowd
Composed of hearts, some good, some proud.
She saw the eager, hungry look,
And from her purse she quickly took

Of glittering pieces not a few ;
Placing in basket, fresh and new,
The nicest things that could be seen
Within dividing glassy screen.
It kept e'en luscious smell away
From passers, who might only stray,
To take a look, but never taste
What often went to sinful waste.

A touch withdraws the child's fixed gaze ;
A few sweet words fill with amaze
The little heart that scarcely knew
The thoughts that, quickly passing through,
Have formed the subject of my verse,
And opened wide the lady's purse.

The bright, full eyes gaze in the face
That looks so full of gentle grace :
" The basket is for you, my child ! " —
" And all that in it I see piled ? "
" Yes, all for you, poor little one ;
Slip it your little arm upon."
The wondering eyes were full of life :
" Oh, tell me ! are you God's 'own' wife ? "

Lady, I never saw thy face ;
Lifted, no doubt, to dwelling-place

Of the Blest Holy One above, —
The Giver of blest Christian love;
But surely thou dost daily seek
Homes the resort of poor and meek.
Forever must those words resound,
As you are daily going round,
And you must see the wondrous light,
And hear the words, " Are you God's wife ? "

Oct. 12, 1865.

To a Soldier's Dog.

FAITHFUL creature, draw thee near me,
    Do not pass me idly by ;
    I would stroke thy shining beauty, —
  I would see thee eye to eye !
I would lay my hand upon thee,
  . As I 've seen another hand,
Lifted proud, or drooping o'er thee,
    For caressing or command !

Faithful creature, draw thee near me,
    Let me touch thy shaggy cheek ;
How I wish, my poor dumb pointer, —
    How I wish that thou couldst speak !
There is soul and there is sorrow
    Beaming in that radiant eye.
Thou hast loved, and thou hast suffered, —
    Draw thee near me, — *so have I.*

Thou hast missed the hand that fed thee,
    And the eye that ever shone,

5

With a brave and manly beauty,
    Kindly, gently on thine own!
Thou hast missed the merry whistle,
    And the hunter's blithesome call,
And the gay, glad, sportive footstep,
    Dearer, dearer than them all!

Draw thee near me; I am weary, —
    Empty places day by day : —
Look into my face, poor pointer;
    What is it that thou wouldst say?
Thou *must* know the hand that fed thee
    Grasps the sabre and the sword;
And the eye that shone upon thee
    Beams to battle's martial word!

Thou *must* know, thy master's footsteps
    High in *danger's* bulwarks stand,
And the voice, the voice that called thee,
    Gives the soldier's loud command!
Thou *must know,* — for something holy,
    Sad and beautiful I see,
In the look of love and pity
    Thou art lifting up to me!

Just as if by wondrous instinct,
    Thou would'st read this heart of mine, —

All the pathos in thy nature
   Kindling in that glance of thine!

Draw thee near me, — many sorrows
   In this vale of tears I've known;
But to-night, beneath the moonlight,
   If I weep, 't is *not alone.*
There is soul and there is sorrow
   Beaming in that radiant eye;
Thou hast loved, and thou hast suffered, —
   Draw thee near me, — *So have I!*

The Lay of the Sunbeam.

I LIE on the mountain as fair and as mild
    As a rose on the breast of an innocent child,
And I hie me, way down to the valley below,
As noiseless and fleet as a spirit could go!
I pierce through the window all darkened by pain,
To bring back the dreamings of gladness again;
And I lay me down softly the cradle beside,
Like a promise of joy to the pathway untried!
I'm in the lone attic, where never a song
Of music or pleasure would seem to belong;
Yet I throw o'er its darkness a glimmer of light
So pensive in beauty, we cling to the sight.
My being is varied: I'm up with the day,
But long before evening I'm passing away;
Yet, changeful and transient, I'm bright to the last,
As a hope in the heart, or a dream in the *past!*

I am lovely and loved, for I come from the sky,
Yet dearer to earth than to heaven am I ;
For I cast the sweet mantle of peace o'er the
    mind,
And leave not a token of sorrow behind !

With my silvery pencil I stroke the blue sea,
And gem the bright waves as they float over me ;
On the white beach I make me a pillow to sleep,
But the gate of the morn 't is my province to
    keep ;
With the gentlest of blushes I garnish its bars,
And dimmed is the light of the glorious stars ;
Then away down the slope of the hill to the
    plain,
I am off on my mission of beauty again !
I stay not a moment, for sweet is my play
With the dew on the grass at the opening of day ;
And the shadow I leave in my beautiful path,
Like the fading of autumn, its radiance hath !

I am sent to the heart-stricken mourner below,
Yet a stranger am I to the anguish of woe ;
No grief have I tasted, no loss have I known,
For I live in the sunshine, — the *sunshine* alone ;
Yet the track of my footstep falls soft 'mid the
    gloom,

As a smile to a tear, so am I to the tomb;
And aloft through the shade of the cypress I
    plant
My beautiful banner all shining aslant!

I fear not the dark-winged angel of Death,
Yet I fly from the storm with its pitiless breath;
E'en the glow of the lightning grows faint on the
    mind,
As I bear my light form on the wings of the
    wind,
And speed like a spirit whose mission is done,
To the " Crown of my Glory," the beautiful Sun!

To a Friend, on her Marriage.

'VE read, that in a distant land there is
    a cherished stone;
    It tells if weal or woe befalls the loved
and absent one;
And as it dims or brightens, the owner's heart
    will be
With fear and hope alternate striving for mastery.

The thought of thee, my friend, with it most
    strangely blends;
Fondly loved, and guarded by parents and by
    friends;
Like it, they would protect thee from all life's
    hurtful things,
And blessing, at the thought of thee, in many a
    bosom springs.

But soon thou wilt be leaving the home of child-
    hood dear,
Another's heart will claim thee, another's home
    thou 'lt cheer;

Then blessings on thee, dear one, — I fain from
    Heaven would crave,
And a Father's hand to guide thee, as life's rude
    storms thou 'lt brave.

Thou hast secured, my gentle girl, that Heavenly
    Father's love,
And I know that thy young heart has found a
    place in world above ;
Then let not life's endearing charms allure thee
    from that troth,
Which solemnly, in angels' view, thou 'st plighted
    in thy youth.

In looking through Time's telescope, I can afar
    perceive
That many joys and sorrows a chain full strong
    will weave ;
And did I not believe thy heart is fixed on joys
    above,
I 'd fear that they might lure thee from thy first,
    thy plighted love.

But now I would not sadden a single hour of joy,
Or at this happy season, Love, impart Fear's dark
    alloy.

That you may both be happy, my earnest prayer
shall rise,
And after life's long journey 's o'er, be welcomed
to the skies.

Our Brother.

A HOME-OFFERING OF LOVE TO THE FIRST-BORN.

WE have woven a wreath for thee, Brother,
    A chaplet of warm, true love,
'Circled with the benison of thy Mother,
    And a blessing from Heaven above !

'T is not composed of bay, Brother,
    The evergreen of Fame ;
Nor of the glistening laurel, Brother,
    They bind on Glory's name !

But 't is inwoven with flowers, Brother, —
    The sweet, the bright, the fair ;
And mingled in its round, Brother,
    The gems of love appear.

There are lilies of fairy tint, Brother,
    Breathing a perfume rare ;
And violets of deepest blue, Brother,
    Shed their rich fragrance there.

The woodbine and the jessamine, Brother,
  Myrtle and holly too,
Combine to form this love-wreath, Brother,
  So bright-hued in its glow.

Thou hast been the blessing of our home,
    Brother,
  With thy warm and loving heart, —
With thy winsome, winning ways, Brother,
  Thy cheerily acted part.

Thou hast gladdened the heart of thy mother,
  Thou hast brightened thy father's brow,
In many a moment of care, Brother,
  In many an hour of woe!

In the home of thy love and cheer, Brother,
  Thy cherished, worshipped home,
Thou hast been the dispenser of joy, Brother,
  The banisher of gloom.

We pray that thy brow may ever, Brother,
  Be crowned with a chaplet of love;
On earth, truth, beauty, and peace be thine,
  And meet thee in heaven above!

April 5th, 1858.

The Present.

LIVE in the *Present.* The Past as a
dream
Is sweet to remember, but yet
The Present, with joys that are real and serene,
Is sweeter, *without a regret.*

The Past was my song in the *days of my youth,*
When fancy is ever so rife,
That the least little care that o'ercloudeth the sun
Seems to darken the whole of the life.

The Past had its friendships, but where are they
now, —
The hearts that so earnestly loved?
Like a bud that is nipped, *a vision that's gone,*
Like a *tale that is told, they have proved.*

Yet the Past I recur to with *pleasure* and *pride;*
I'm grateful *e'en where she deceived;*
She enlivened my life in the days that are gone,
And her sorrows are *more than retrieved.*

For the Present hath joys which she promised
   me not,
Whose halo around me is cast,
Too brightly to yield *to a shade of regret*
   In view of the treacherous Past.

Judge not.

 UDGE not! for you may say a word,
    That you scarce deem one soul has
      heard;
Judge not! a loving heart may bleed,
Because your words, like lightning speed,
May as electric shock be brought,
To agonize by wounded thought
Some heart, all innocent and pure,
Leaving it innocent no more.

For that poor heart may curse the tongue
That sent its poisoned dart upon
A victim that ne'er dreamed of wrong,
Or could to such a class belong, —
Whose vilest judgment makes appear
The injured one foul wrong to share.
Then judge no one by heart, by tongue:
Truth is not judgment; and upon
A fact becoming known as true,
Do to that neighbor e'en what you

Would wish in your own case might be
Done to your *loved*, or else to *thee*.

If we the golden rule would keep,
How rich a harvest we would reap
Of grateful words, of smiles, of love,
And what is precious far above
All pleasures which our senses know, —
And which we never could forego,
If once we tasted the rich pleasure
Of gaining from our Lord the treasure
Of a pure heart, all free from guile,
Gladdened by its Creator's smile.

Who, who can gently look above,
And say, O God, my life is love?
Who can unblushingly behold
All men in thought stand near enrolled,
And feel no bitter, taunting word
Has ever from the lips been heard;
No gentle spirit wounds has felt,
No tears from burning lids did melt,
Because harsh, thoughtless words have sped
To homes where innocence has fled,
To hide the burning cheek from scorn,
And wish for night, and then for morn?

Let us remember that to judge
   Is 'gainst the will of Heaven!
That to be judged we must expect,
   Unless we firm have striven
Against the sin so prone to all, —
To think that those who seem to fall,
Must for peculiar sin be tried,
That thus they may be *sanctified.*

Oct. 13*th*, 1865.

Such is Life.

SHE stood beside me in the hour
    When plighted vows were made,
    And seemed like a transplanted flower
  From Eden's sunny glade;
So bright she was! her brow without
  The shadow of a shade.

Love was the watchword of her soul;
  And one was by her side,
Who hoped ere long to claim her as
  His cherished, chosen bride.
No cloud above their happiness;
  But oh! he could not see
The darkness that was gathering,
  Alas! so fearfully.

These loving hearts so pure, so true,
  Were destined to be riven;
The summons was upon its way,
    The charge already given,

Which was to bear his soul from earth,
　I fondly trust, to heaven.

And thus he left her; one short year
　Of wedded bliss was theirs;
It opened bright with smiles of hope,
　It closed with bitter tears.
But oh, amidst this night of gloom,
　One ray of joy appears:
How precious was that baby smile,
　How sweet his cooing tone!
And soon his little voice would learn
　To call the absent one;
But no, another message came, —
　The mother was alone.

Alone? Oh, no! her trust is there,
　Where both her loved ones dwell;
She hears them in the Better Land
　The angel chorus swell;
And while she weeps, she ever says,
　God "doeth all things well."

Our Pastor.

DEATH has often been amongst us,
　　Bringing sadness to the heart;
　Often have our souls in anguish
Bowed beneath his cruel dart.

But oh, never, never, never
　Such a visit as the last!
Never hath his presence o'er us
　Such a midnight sorrow cast.

Now his summons has deprived us
　Of our pastor and our friend, —
Brought the sweetest earthly union
　To a sudden, dreadful end.

Oh! what shall we do without thee?
　Who can ever fill thy place?
Who, in strength of mind and learning,
　Who, in spiritual grace?

Who, in tenderness of manner?
　Who, in sympathy of soul?
We may chance to find a portion,
　But we never can the whole.

Who in love shall stand beside us,
　To bestow the bread of life?
Who shall comfort and console us
　In its sorrow and its strife?

God hath done it, and in wisdom
　He may choose another head;
But our hearts can never love him
　As they loved the precious dead.

The Guardian Angel.

Lines suggested by hearing of the protection granted to a house and family, when, on the soldiery entering the house to plunder, the young mother pointed to the beautiful corpse of her child, and exclaimed, " Let this be our protection!"

HOME desolate! the bright, bright eyes
Are closed, to open in the skies.
The cherub lips are firmly pressed,
Each little hand is on the breast;
The little feet, that wandered o'er
Fields, woods, and home, must never more
Be pressed on early falling dew,
Nor paths bright scattered, through and through,
With flowers and petals of gayest hue.

There lies the angel of the dwelling;
Hidden are hearts with anguish swelling;
Tears like the purest crystal dew
Fall on the marble form anew;

They take oppression from the breast,
They teach the weary brain to rest.

Silence is broken ; rude, strong hand
Throws wide the door to soldier band ;
Fierce eyes flash on the tear-stained faces,
Then feet seem rooted to their places ;
For firm, firm voice commands their ear,
And steady eyes evince no fear.
A mother's voice will touch the heart,
And maké those cruel foes depart.

Stop ! she exclaims, in voice decisive,
And looks returned are not derisive.
Stop !—and the voice breathes forth affec-
    tion, —
Look there ! *Let that be our protection !*

Those men, who came to burn and sack,
Looked pityingly, and then turned back.
" Protect this house," was the command.
" Let guards be stationed, that no band
May enter, to disturb by tread
This *home made sacred by the dead.*"

And though the sounds of war were near,
Silence was broken there by prayer.

And ever in those loving hearts,
As, year by year Old Time departs,
Will that pure, lovely child be known
As Guardian Angel of its Home.

Oct. 1865.

Lines

ON THE DEATH OF THE WRITER OF THE "VILLAGE CHURCH,"

Who died at his home in Savannah, just after his return from Harvard University, aged twenty years.

 EARTH, how many bright ones
Are in thy bosom laid!
How many kindred spirits
Now seek their home in thy dark caverns!
Death! thou dost find thy victims
Amongst earth's rarest and most gifted children,
And now thou hast taken *One*,
Who blossomed forth so fair, so beautiful,
So full of taste and talent, gentleness and love,
That every heart sinks at the sudden, awful change,
And every eye grows dim with sickening tears!

But who can tell a father's woe, a father's anguish,
In this dreary, dark, and dreaded hour?
Who can feel the crush of all the hopes of gathering years,

Who can tell the sickening woe that reigns,
Where lived, in all the pride of youth,
And all the promise of his early years,
The gifted son ?
O most tried parent ! all other grief sinks before
    thine.
So mightily it presses on thy heart,
That, should the spring of life itself give way,
    We would not wonder.

But oh ! remember, in this trying hour,
That *He who gave*, has taken away !
That He has claimed *His own*,
Which, but for a little time, *He lent to thee !*
    Bless thou His name !
And while thy heart, in deepest woe,
Feels the full agony of this His act,
Bend it, though it should break,
To His most mighty will :
Then will the light burst forth ;
Then will the darkness disappear ;
And He who while on earth did raise the dead,
Shall, in the resurrection,
    Raise thy son !

Before the War.

Written on " seeing " a mother fall asleep, after talking over
anxieties about her sons, who, together with their father,
were in the Confederate service. Only two were together.

LEEP on, dear troubled one !
Sleep on ! in sweet unconsciousness ;
Dream dreams, that bring your little
ones back to your side.
See their bright eyes, glancing and dancing
Midst bright beds of curls.
Look at their coral lips ; smile as you hear them
speak of deeds of daring,
Which they 'll accomplish when they shall be men.
Laugh to behold them, with stern soldier air,
Making of broom a gun, of wood a spear.
See how they brandish, with an innate grace,
their little swords,
As they through exercises go.
See their eyes flash, hear tones of triumph.
Now they flush, for they have buried glittering
blade in heart of foe,
Or stricken from his hated trunk his head by
well-aimed blow.

Ah! little did you think that every dash
Made by your darling boys was fitting them for
    war, —
Little dream, that, when you sent them shoeless
    on sweet ——'s sands,
It was to teach them to endure toils in store, —
    Obedience to commands.

Sleep on! Heaven guard your treasures ;
Heaven grant that sweet, sweet pleasures
Are laid in keeping, for your absent ones.
Sleep on! Dry off, ye tears scarce shed for hus-
    bands, sons.
Sleep on! sleep on! sleep on!

After the War.

WAKE up! wake up! we *must not* sleep!
We must scarce take the time to weep.
We must look ills of life in face,
And keep our energies apace.
For we must a new life begin,
And try to live, to crush out sin.

Wake, mother! wake! and smile anew!
All the loved band are safely through;
Life, limbs, and brain, all, all are saved,
And eyes may open without grave
And silent darkness staring through,
On objects that the earth still strew,
Never to be beheld again,
With wonder, love, or even pain.

Wake, mother! to the toils of life;
Wake to endure the daily strife
Which poverty will bring to those

Whose paling cheek with crimson glows,
As they are learning lesson sad,
That even comforts must be had
By struggling daily, nightly too,
To get the plainest fare anew.

Wake, mother, wake! your faith is firm, —
You have not now blest faith to learn;
You can with patience struggle on,
And bid your heart in God be strong.
For sons are called, as manhood's cares
Cluster around with hopes and fears,
To dedicate themselves anew
To Father, who, all through and through,
Has gently placed restraining hand
Upon that mother's little band,
Taking the wounded in His care,
Giving the sick a goodly share
Of kind attention and of love,
From all below, and from above.

Mother, awake! you 're blessed of God;
The darkest path ere this is trod.
What can we dread when He is ours?
Ne'er Death, or Hell, or earthly powers.
Tired, you 'll think of *rest forever;*
Rested, you 'll think of time when never

Shall *anxious weariness* be felt,
For all in love combined shall melt,
Forming a contrast passing strange,
Which none but God can e'er arrange.

Oct. 14th, 1865.

Lines

TO A YELLOW JESSAMINE PRESSED FOR A FRIEND

SWEET vine! that lov'st in graceful
    folds to twine
    Around the stately oak or lofty pine,
To fling thy garlands gay from tree to tree,
In sportive forms, so wild, so sweet, so free.

Thy golden flowers in massive richness seen,
Mingling with moss and various tints of green,
Shedding sweet fragrance on each vernal gale
Which gently wafts it through the woody vale.

Though torn from parent stem, and rudely
    pressed,
Thy lifeless form will still in beauty rest;
And bring to sleeping memory the clime
Where jessamines grow wild, and warm suns
    shine.

Lines

ADDRESSED BY AN OFFICER TO THREE LADIES, ON RE-
CEIVING FROM THEM A PRESENT OF A PAIR OF
CUFFS.

OH, sweet memento, but perplexing sight!
Behold the sorrows of a luckless wight!
Cuffed by fierce foes, and cuffed by
smiling friends,
His sorrows deepen, and his gloom extends.
The prison chill but late bedamped his brow,
And friendly wishes rest upon it now;
Behold a quandary in which to stand, —
A suffering soldier, cuffed on either hand.

But like the Christian, who, with patience meek,
Presents the smiter with alternate cheek,
So will the soldier, humble still, though rough,
His " arms present " for every graceful cuff, —
Will wield those arms for Southern homes and
rights,
Receive the cuffs, and bless the hand that smites.

AUGUSTA, *Ga.*, 1862.

Lines

THERE is an unobtrusive flower,
　　Filling with fragrance tree and bower;
　　Its modest, blushing color lies
In pale, pale pink, and deepest dyes
Of the same shade, till o'er is spread
Its brightest tint of rosy red.

Methinks no passing one could tread
Regardless by, when perfume shed
Like luscious, tempting fruit is brought
By gentle breeze, which tree has sought;
A look would wander overhead,
And search for source whence fragrance fled.

But you must quietly regard
That delicate tree.　Do not retard
By hasty touch the flowing sap;
For unaware you thus, mayhap,
May make the exquisite leaves of green
Wither, 'neath touch almost unseen.

7

So with the sensitive flowers of life;
They wither 'neath e'en words of strife;
They shrink as if the heart is dead;
Paleness o'er delicate tints is spread,
Often by unreflecting word,
Or murmur that is scarcely heard.

Look gently, and let no rude touch
Descend upon e'en natures such.
Defend them from the careless word,
Defend them from keen sarcasm heard,
Defend them from the ills of life,
Defend them from harsh words of strife.

For many a trembling nature shrinks
Into *itself*, and, trembling, thinks
That it is useless to pretend
To struggle, or try to defend
A heart that shrinks, and shrinks again,
When felt is *own and others' pain.*

Oct. 15th, 1865.

To the Old Year.

FAREWELL, Old Year! We look with
    sadness back,
    And see thy dark and dreary blood-
stained track.
We seem to think of thee when thou art o'er,
As shipwrecked ones regard the distant shore.
We hope, and yet we hope as blind ones may
Hope for the beams of bright and gladdening
    day.
We trust, for we ere this dark paths have trod,
Which led us, *strangely*, to our Father, God.
We bless, for blessed is that Father's hand,
Guiding us from the cheats, — the smooth quick-
    sand.
We ask forgiveness, for full well we know
We 've well *deserved* a fiercer, heavier blow.

Farewell, Old Year! Hide deep within your
    breast
All of our anguish and our dread unrest ;

Let us remember our blest noble brave,
And drop with laurels tears upon each grave.
Let us remember that the days draw nigh,
When we shall speak of them with *smile*, not
　　sigh.
Forever shall the sad, the blighted past
Be sacred to us, — as the shadows cast
Their pall upon the things gone quickly by,
Covering each tear-drop, and each heart's deep
　　sigh.

Farewell, Old Year! and welcome to the New!
Sadly we 've borne the past, but it is through.
Brighter the day, when blackest clouds have
　　sped,
Like winged messengers, bearing off their dead, —
Leaving the sky from gloomy shadows freed,
Hasting to earth with gladness and with speed!
Frowning upon us first with clouded face,
Then kissing flowers and greens, in whose em-
　　brace
We see our Father's tender, pitying love
In glimpses of the joys in store above.

Welcome, New Year! Bring peace on softest
　　wing;
Oh, cry not *Peace*, and leave the latent sting!

Come to us with a sweet, a smiling face :
Smiles, *if sincere*, true heart can ne'er disgrace.
Come ! gently woo us from depression's weights ;
Come ! take oppression from our homes, — our
    States ;
Then, though we *sadly* bid thee welcome now,
We 'll in the end kiss *warmly* thy fair brow.

SAVANNAH, *Dec. 11th*, 1865.